DOVER PUBLICATIONS, INC.
MINEOLA, NEW YORK

...cked pages ...ny me...a you like, and make display...g you... finished work easy!

Bibliographical Note

Mermaids Coloring Book is a new work, first published
by Dover Publications, Inc., in 2016.

International Standard Book Number

ISBN-13: 978-0-486-80943-4
ISBN-10: 0-486-80943-9

Manufactured in the United States by LSC Communications
80943907   2017
www.doverpublications.com